For Susan
—M. I. B.

For my dad, always young at heart
—D. R. O.

ACKNOWLEDGMENTS

The illustrator thanks Justin Chanda, Laurent Linn, and Dani Young at
Simon & Schuster Children's for helping to make the creative process so much FUN.

SIMON & SCHUSTER BOOKS FOR YOUNG READERS
An imprint of Simon & Schuster Children's Publishing Division
1230 Avenue of the Americas, New York, New York 10020
Text copyright © 2014 by Hot Schwartz Productions
Illustrations copyright © 2014 by Debbie Ridpath Ohi
All rights reserved, including the right of reproduction in whole or in part in any form.
SIMON & SCHUSTER BOOKS FOR YOUNG READERS is a trademark of Simon & Schuster, Inc.
For information about special discounts for bulk purchases, please contact Simon & Schuster Special Sales
at 1-866-506-1949 or business@simonandschuster.com.
The Simon & Schuster Speakers Bureau can bring authors to your live event. For more information or to book an event,
contact the Simon & Schuster Speakers Bureau at 1-866-248-3049 or visit our website at www.simonspeakers.com.
Book design by Laurent Linn
The text for this book is set in Hank BT.
The illustrations for this book are rendered digitally.
Manufactured in China
0214 SCP
2 4 6 8 10 9 7 5 3 1
Library of Congress Cataloging-in-Publication Data
Black, Michael Ian.
Naked! / Michael Ian Black ; illustrated by Debbie Ridpath Ohi. — First edition.
pages cm
Summary: A child discovers that the only thing more fun than being naked is wearing nothing but a cape.
ISBN 978-1-4424-6738-5 (hardcover : alk. paper) — ISBN 978-1-4424-6739-2 (ebook) [1. Nudity—Fiction.
2. Clothing and dress—Fiction. 3. Humorous stories.] I. Ohi, Debbie Ridpath, 1962– illustrator. II. Title.
PZ7.B5292Nak 2014
[E]—dc23
2013016383

NAKED!

Michael Ian Black

ILLUSTRATED BY
Debbie Ridpath Ohi

SIMON & SCHUSTER BOOKS FOR YOUNG READERS

New York   London   Toronto   Sydney   New Delhi

Look at me, everybody!

I'm **naked**!

Sliding

down

the

stairs

naked!

Eating a **cookie** totally and completely naked!

I should dress like this

all the time.

I could go to school **naked.**

Play on the playground **naked.**

Do the Hokey Pokey

naked.

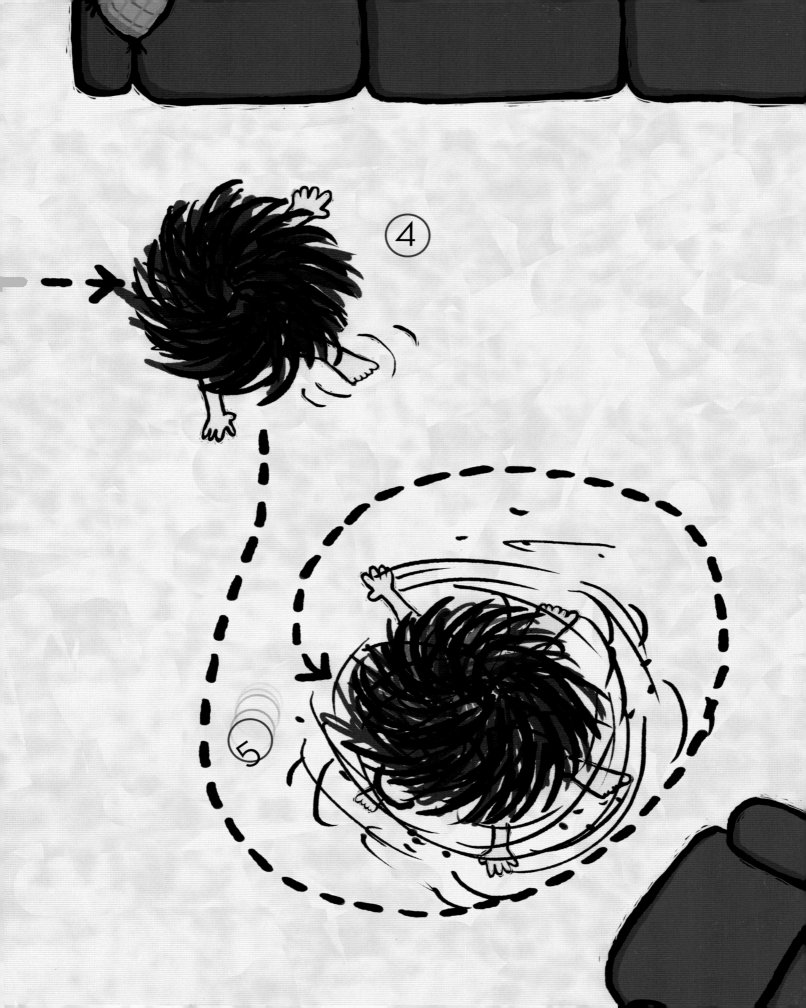

Pants?

Who needs pants?

Or shirts

or shoes

or capes.

Fighting evildoers

caped!

bad guys'
HeadQuarters

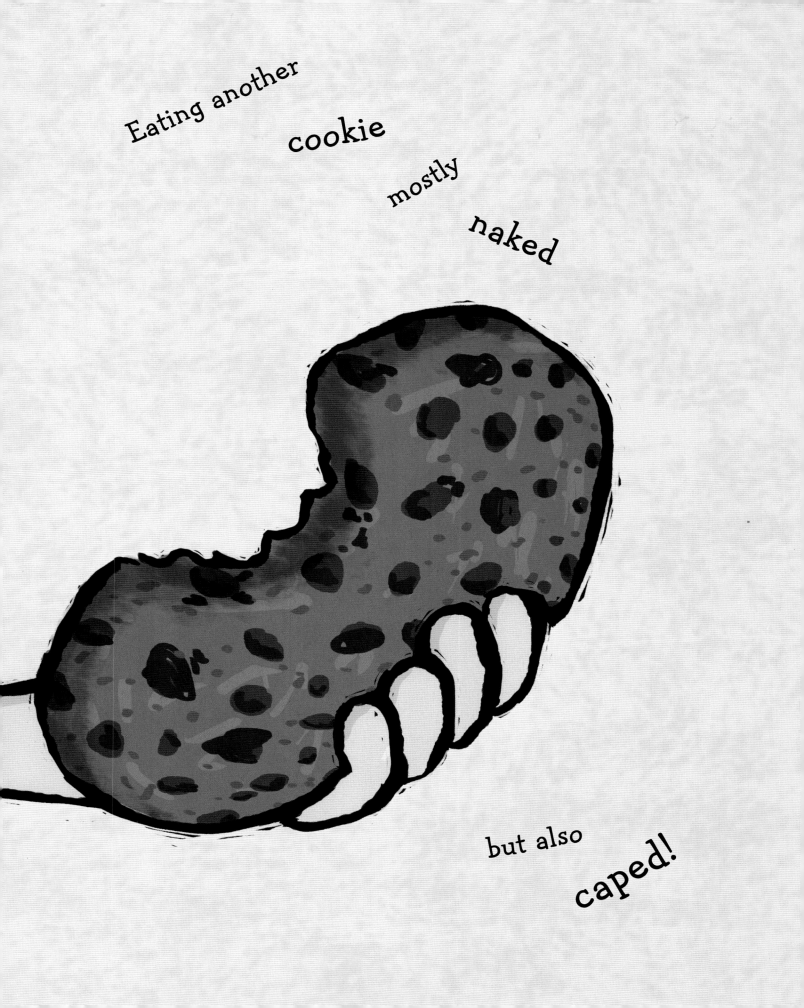

Being naked is great,

but being

caped

is even

better!

Except that now I'm . . .

Sneaking

downstairs

cold.

Eating one last cookie

cold.

Maybe I should put on some pants.

And a top.

And maybe these slippers.

And maybe take off the cape.

And now I am . . .

exhausted.

And now I am . . .

asleep.